Tien 11/16

← YOU CHOOSE →

SCOOBY-DOO!

THE CASE OF THE FRIGHT FLIGHT

STONE ARCH BOOKS
a capstone imprint

You Choose Stories: Scooby-Doo
is published by Stone Arch Books,
A Capstone Imprint
1710 Roe Crest Drive
North Mankato, Minnesota 56003
www.mycapstone.com

CAPS34910

Cataloging-in-Publication Data is available on the
Library of Congress website.
ISBN: 978-1-4965-2662-5 [Library Hardcover]
ISBN: 978-1-4965-2664-9 [Paperback]
ISBN: 978-1-4965-2666-3 [eBook]

Printed in the United States of America in North Mankato, Minnesota.
092015   009221CGS16

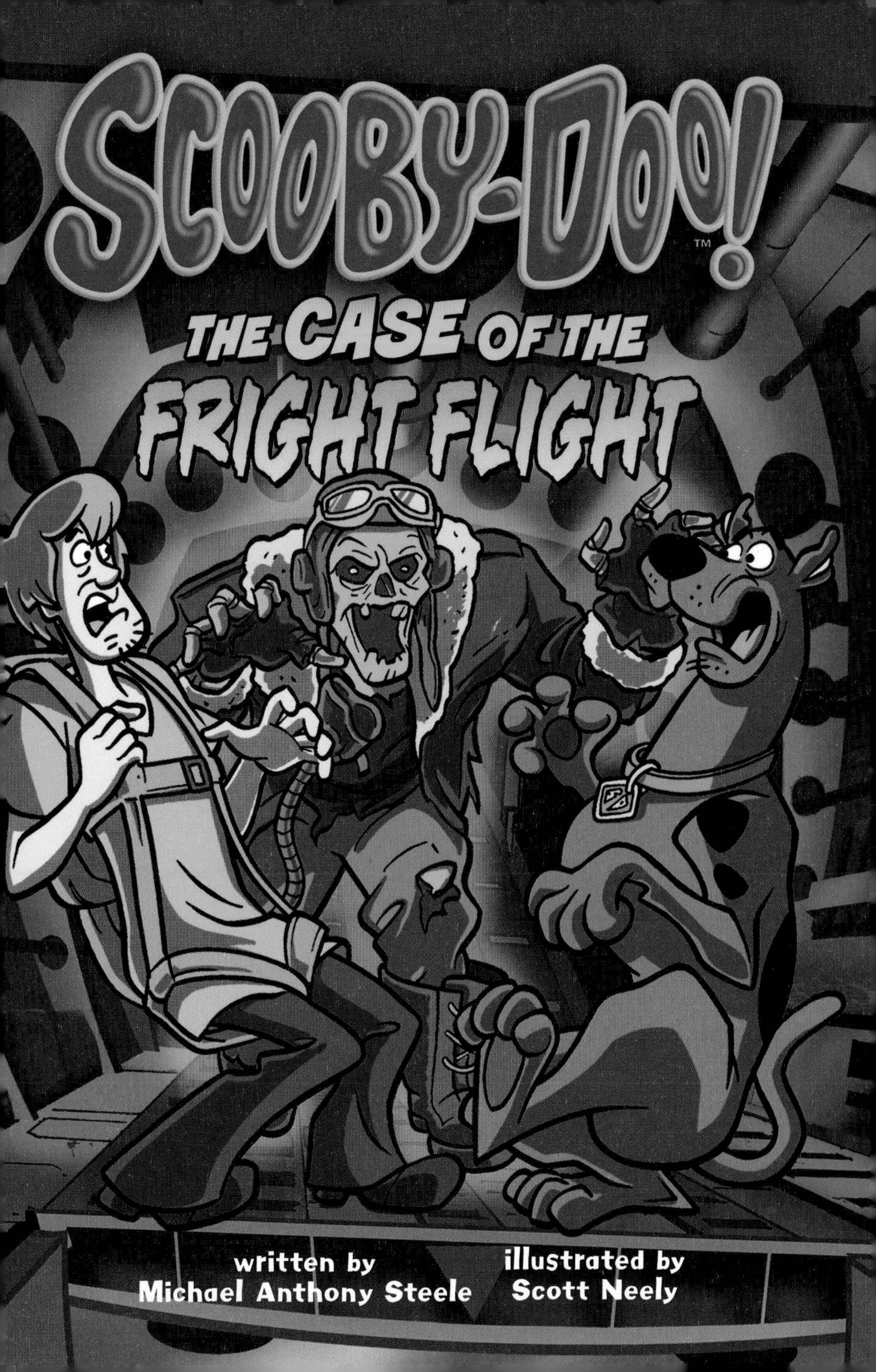
SCOOBY-DOO!™
THE CASE OF THE
FRIGHT FLIGHT
written by
Michael Anthony Steele
illustrated by
Scott Neely

THE MYSTERY INC. GANG!

SCOOBY-DOO

SKILLS: Loyal; super snout
BIO: This happy-go-lucky hound avoids
scary situations at all costs, but he'll do
anything for a Scooby Snack!

SHAGGY ROGERS

SKILLS: Lucky; healthy appetite
BIO: This laid-back dude would rather
look for grub than search for clues,
but he usually finds both!

FRED JONES, JR.

SKILLS: Athletic; charming
BIO: The leader and oldest member
of the gang. He's a good sport—and good
at them, too!

DAPHNE BLAKE

SKILLS: Brains; beauty
BIO: As a sixteen-year-old fashion queen,
Daphne solves her mysteries in style.

VELMA DINKLEY

SKILLS: Clever; highly intelligent
BIO: Although she's the youngest member
of Mystery Inc., Velma's an old pro at
catching crooks.

SCOOBY-DOO!

Who or what is haunting the hangar at Kevin Ryan's spectacular air show? Who's behind the appearance of the mysterious World War II bomber the *Silver Hawk*? Only YOU can help Scooby-Doo and the Mystery Inc. gang solve the mystery.

Follow the directions at the bottom of each page. The choices YOU make will change the outcome of the story. After you finish one path, go back and read the others for more Scooby-Doo adventures!

YOU CHOOSE the path to solve...

THE **CASE** OF THE
FRIGHT FLIGHT

The Mystery Inc. gang sits in a row and looks to the sky. All together, their heads turn left. Then right. Then their heads spin around in a loop-the-loop.

"Ruh-roh," Scooby-Doo says. "I'm retting rizzy!" Scooby places a paw on each side of his head. He stops his head from moving but his eyes spin like pinwheels.

"You said it, pal," Shaggy agrees. "I feel a little dizzy myself." **GURRRRRGLE!** Shaggy holds his stomach. "And like, maybe I shouldn't have eaten that tenth hot dog."

The gang is watching an air show. While the crowd watches from bleachers, colorful stunt planes soar overhead. The airplanes climb high into the sky. They dive, twirl, and loop.

Turn the page.

"Ten hot dogs is an awful lot, Shaggy." Velma shakes her head. "Even for you."

"Like, Kevin said it was all you could eat at the concession stand," Shaggy explains. "Sounded like a challenge to me!"

"Ree, too!" Scooby agrees, giggling with a mouth full of popcorn.

Kevin Ryan, a friend of the Mystery Inc. gang, has invited them to an exciting air show at his airfield. All afternoon, the spectators have marveled at the antics of stunt planes and flybys of historical aircraft. Even a large blimp, like a giant hot-air balloon, lumbers across the sky.

The stunt planes make one more pass over the crowd. Everyone claps as the planes leave trails of smoke across the sky. Then, one by one, the planes touch down on the long runway.

"Let's give it up for Rocket Rodney Harrison!" the announcer's voice barks from the loudspeakers. "And his Rainbow Rockets stunt team!"

The audience applauds as the last plane lands. Then, several trucks drive onto the runway.

Daphne nudges Fred. "A great way to spend your birthday, huh?"

"You said it," Fred agrees. Then he points to the open airfield. "Look. They're setting up for Kevin's air race."

The work crews drop off large bundles onto the landing strip. Then one of the crew members pulls a cord and the bundles inflate. Soon, several huge cones are scattered around the airfield.

"What are they doing?" asks Daphne.

"Those giant cones are called pylons," Fred explains. "The pilots fly between and around them during the race."

Velma smiles. "And the pilot who flies around them the fastest wins."

Shaggy gulps. "Sounds dangerous."

"It can be," Fred replies. "But wait until you see it. It's very exciting!"

Turn the page.

Velma eyes a run-down hangar on the far end of the airfield. "As exciting as a visit to the haunted hangar?"

Scooby's popcorn goes flying. "Raunted Rangar?!!"

"Like, what is that?" Shaggy asks. His eyes are wide with fright.

Velma laughs. "If you two weren't at the concession stand for so long, you would have heard all about it."

"Kevin tells us it's an old hangar that no one uses," Daphne explains. "His mechanic, Dan, and some of the other workers call it the haunted hangar."

"Ladies and gentlemen!" the announcer's voice blasts from the loudspeakers. "First up in the air race today . . . let's hear it for Dirk Wilson!"

The audience applauds as a small black plane taxis onto the runway. Its propeller roars as it lines up and takes off.

The plane soars into the sky and then turns back toward the first pair of pylons. It flies through, beginning the race. It continues turning on each side as it zigzags in between the line of giant cones. "*Oooh!*" says the audience all together. "*Aaaaaah!*"

"*Rooooh!*" says Scooby-Doo. "*Raaaaaah!*"

The plane straightens up and zips between two more pylons. It shoots high into the sky, turns, and flies through the same course in reverse. When the plane darts between the last two pylons, the race is over. The small black plane comes in for a landing.

"54.15 seconds!" shouts the announcer.

"You were right, Fred." Daphne applauds along with the rest of the audience. "That was exciting."

Velma points to a small red plane rolling onto the field. "There's Kevin."

The loudspeaker crackles. "And now, the undefeated champion, Kevin Ryan!"

Turn the page.

Kevin's plane takes off and races into the sky. It slowly turns and lines up with the first set of pylons. The plane then darts down the middle and then it spins and zigzags between the others, just as Dirk had done.

"Is he going faster?" asks Daphne.

Velma scrunches up her eyes. "It's hard to tell."

As Kevin's plane rockets through the last set of large cones, the audience is stone silent.

"53.51 seconds!" yells the announcer. "Kevin Ryan wins again!"

Everyone cheers as Kevin comes in for a landing. Work crews race onto the field and begin deflating the giant cones. Kevin climbs out of his plane and joins the Mystery Inc. gang.

"What did you guys think?" asks Kevin.

Fred gives him a thumbs-up. "That was amazing!"

"Res, really ramazing!" agrees Scooby-Doo.

A brown-haired woman with a video camera marches up to the bleachers. She points the camera at Kevin. "What were you thinking during that last turn, Kevin?"

Kevin smiles. "What I always think about, Sheila. Not crashing." He points to the landing strip below. "But enough about me. I think you'll want your crew to shoot the grand finale."

Sheila winks at him. "You got it." She marches back down the bleachers.

"Who was that?" asks Velma.

"That's Sheila Wilcox," Kevin replies. "She's filming a reality show about our airfield. They get in the way sometimes, but you get used to them."

"So that's why there are camera operators all over the place," Daphne says.

Turn the page.

The loudspeaker crackles. "Ladies and gentlemen. Before the sun sets, we have one more aircraft to show you."

On the airfield below, a large plane lumbers onto the landing strip. Four sets of propellers rumble as it taxis down the runway. A large silver bird is painted on its nose.

"During World War II, a B-17 bomber named the *Silver Hawk* disappeared without a trace," says the announcer. "Thanks to Kevin Ryan and his mechanic, Dan Erickson, we can show you what the bomber looked like. Behold, a detailed replica of the *Silver Hawk* will now fly off into the sunset."

"We've been building it for a year," Kevin explains. "I can't wait to see it fly."

POW! A large puff of smoke bursts from one of the engines. The plane rolls to a stop.

Velma covers her mouth. "Oh, no! What happened?"

Kevin shakes his head. "I don't know."

"Like, that's not all," says Shaggy. "Look."

A large cloud of white fog drifts over the airfield. It fills the sky, and then something pushes its way out of it. A large plane emerges. Its body is tattered and the paint is dull. But a familiar symbol is painted on the nose—a silver hawk.

Kevin's eyes widen. "The *Silver Hawk!*"

"Like, the real *Silver Hawk?*" Shaggy asks. "A g-g-ghost plane?!!"

Scooby's ears droop. "Ruh-roh!"

Scooby and Shaggy hug each other while they shiver with fright.

The large plane glides silently overhead. The audience runs screaming from the bleachers. Even the camera crew flees. Soon, only Kevin and the Mystery Inc. gang remain.

Turn the page.

Daphne points to the plane as it drifts off into the sunset. "Look. It's flying away."

"It's heading for the airplane graveyard," explains Kevin.

Shaggy's teeth chatter louder. "T-t-tell me you didn't say 'graveyard'?"

"It's not a real graveyard," says Kevin. "That's what they call a place that has a bunch of parked airplanes that can no longer fly. We try to repair some of the planes. But mainly we just use them for parts."

Fred turns to the others and grins. "What a great birthday present, gang . . . a real mystery!" He hops to his feet. "Let's split up and see what's going on!"

To investigate the haunted hangar with Velma, turn to page 62.

To follow Shaggy and Scooby to the bomber, turn to page 69.

To check out the airplane graveyard with Fred and Daphne, turn to page 26.

Velma searches everywhere for her glasses. She has to find them before the ghost pilots find her.

Suddenly, a chill runs down her spine. A cold hand takes one of Velma's outstretched hands. The hand slowly places Velma's hand onto her glasses. Velma snatches up her glasses and scrambles backward. When she puts her glasses on, the two blurs in front of her transform into Fred and Daphne.

"Jinkies, Fred," says Velma. "You almost gave me a heart attack."

Fred holds a finger over his lips. "*Shhhh.* There are ghost pilots all over this place," he whispers.

"They're super creepy," Daphne adds.

"I know," says Velma. "I saw one . . . up close and personal."

"What are they doing here?" asks Daphne.

Velma shakes her head. "I don't know. But a bunch of them were gathered together on the other side of the hangar."

"Let's go check it out," Fred suggests.

Velma, Fred, and Daphne creep to the other side of the hangar. Several times, they have to hide behind a piece of equipment as a ghost pilot shambles by. Finally, they reach a large object covered with a white tarp.

"This is it," says Velma.

Fred pulls up the tarp to reveal a black airplane underneath.

"What do ghosts want with an airplane?" asks Daphne.

Velma sniffs the air. "An airplane with fresh paint."

"Someone's coming," Fred whispers. Green glows approach from all sides.

Turn to page 74.

Shaggy and Scooby follow their noses through the dark woods. Soon they discover a campsite with a roaring campfire. Two whole chickens roast above the fire on a long skewer. **RRRRRUMBLE!** Scooby and Shaggy's stomachs growl when they smell the tasty food.

"Boy, that smells good." Shaggy rubs his stomach. "Like, do you think anyone will notice if we take a bite?"

Scooby doesn't reply.

"Scoobs?" asks Shaggy. He turns to see that Scooby-Doo is gone. "Scooby-Doo?" Shaggy whispers. "Where are you?"

Shaggy looks back at the campsite to see his pal sneaking up to the campfire. Before Shaggy can catch up, Scooby-Doo grabs the skewer. The dog holds the long rod above his mouth and the chickens slide down. The first one pops into his waiting mouth.

"Hang on, Scoobs!" Shaggy has just enough time to snag a drumstick off the second chicken before it falls into Scooby's mouth, too.

"Like, what happened to share and share alike?" asks Shaggy.

Scooby's ears droop. "Rorry." He rubs his stomach. "I was rungry."

Shaggy shrugs. "At least I got a drumstick." He takes a big bite.

Shaggy hears footsteps in the woods. With the drumstick still in his mouth, Shaggy dives behind a large bush. He looks around for Scooby-Doo but can't spot him. Shaggy sees the back end of Scooby poking out of a large ice chest. The footsteps grow louder.

"Scooby! Someone's coming!" Shaggy tries to say. But he still has the drumstick in his mouth. Instead, it sounds like, "*Mmmm! Mmm-mmm mmm-mmm!*"

Turn the page.

Shaggy removes the drumstick and is about to warn his friend for real. He freezes in terror when he sees two more ghost pilots moving between the trees. They each have glowing faces and hands and wear raggedy flight suits. They slowly creep toward the campsite.

"Zoinks!" Shaggy's lips quiver. "These woods are haunted!"

Scooby doesn't see them. The dog's head is still deep inside the ice chest. Scooby must have found a tasty treat because he chews loudly. **CHOMP! CHOMP! CHOMP!**

The ghosts move closer and closer. They step into the campsite. The light from the campfire dances over their ghoulish faces.

Scooby continues to eat something inside the ice chest. **CHOMP! CHOMP! CHOMP! CHOMP!**

"Oh, no!" Shaggy whispers. "The ghosts are going to nab my bestest buddy!" Then the ghosts stop in their tracks. One of them points to Scooby-Doo.

Instead of going after Scooby, the pointing ghost tugs at his face. He pulls off a ghost mask. It's just a man wearing a ghost costume.

"A wild animal!" shouts the man. "I'm outta here!" He turns and runs for it.

The "ghosts" fumble into each other before tearing off back into the woods.

Shaggy springs out from behind the bush. "Come on, Scoobs. We got the ghosts on the run. And they're not ghosts after all!" He takes off after the galloping ghouls.

Scooby pulls his head out of the ice chest. A long string of sausages dangles from his mouth. He slurps up the sausages as if they were a long strand of spaghetti. He smacks his lips. "Reee-ricious!"

Scooby glances around the campsite. "Raggy?" He spots his friend running into the dark woods. "Raggy!" Scooby's legs start moving before he does. "Rait for me!"

Turn the page.

Shaggy and Scooby chase the phony ghosts through the trees. They finally catch up to the ghost pilots near the edge of the forest. The fake ghosts speed past another man. The third man wears a suit and a top hat.

"Wait, you can't leave," says the man in the hat. He waves his arms but the ghosts keep running.

"You're not paying us enough for this," says one of the pilots. They leave the man and run back toward the airfield.

Shaggy and Scooby skid to a stop. "Like, what's going on here?" Shaggy asks. "Those aren't real ghosts!"

The man removes his hat and scratches his head. "True. True. I'm Terry Stephenson, theme park owner." He points to the airfield. "I wanted to show Mr. Ryan how he could turn his airfield into a fright park during Halloween."

"Those ghost pilots were pretty scary," Shaggy admits. "But like, what about the ghost plane?"

Mr. Stephenson smiles. "Ah! My favorite!" He leads Shaggy and Scooby out of the woods to the edge of the airfield. A large pack connected to metal tanks sits in the grass. "Observe!"

Stephenson pulls a cord on the pack and it begins to inflate. **HISSSSSSS!** Soon a full-sized ghost plane floats above them.

"Just like the pylons for the air race," says Shaggy.

"Exactly," agrees Stephenson.

"Let's go back," Shaggy suggests. "Maybe Kevin will like your idea when we tell him how scary it really is. And, believe me, we know about scary."

Scooby nods and giggles. "Reah! We know arout rary!"

THE END

To follow another path, turn to page 17.

Fred and Daphne run across the airfield. They slow to a walk when they reach the first old plane. They move past it to see dozens of other old planes lined in several rows. Some planes are missing wings, tails, and even cockpits. There are many huge piles of airplane parts between some of the rows of planes. The mini junkyards and neglected airplanes look eerie in the pale moonlight. Fred and Daphne have found the airplane graveyard.

"I know it's not a real graveyard," Daphne says, "but it still looks pretty creepy."

"No kidding," Fred agrees.

Daphne fishes a flashlight from her purse. She shines the beam in front of them as they move down one of the rows.

Daphne leads the way as she and Fred turn down another row. Fred stops and points to something ahead of them.

"What's that?" asks Fred.

Daphne aims the flashlight at a shadow beside one of the planes. It looks like a tattered jumpsuit hanging from the side of the plane.

"That's an old World War II flight suit," she explains. "The kind bomber crews wore." She moves the beam of light up the suit's tattered legs, waist, and then chest.

"I don't think that's just a suit," says Fred. "I think someone's wearing it."

When Daphne's flashlight beam moves past the chest, she sees that Fred is right. The beam lights up a ghostly face. The pale green face stares back at them with hollow black eyes and a gaping mouth.

"Is th-th-th-that a . . .," Daphne begins to ask.

"A ghost!" Fred finishes for her.

The ghoul in the shredded flight suit moans. It reaches out its glowing green hands and lunges for them.

"Run!" Daphne shouts.

Turn to page 64.

Velma searches until she spots a thin metal ladder. She quietly climbs up, up, and up. When she's near the ceiling, she carefully steps onto one of the narrow catwalks. **CREEEEAK**. The rusty metal walkway creaks and moans with every step.

"Good thing I'm not scared of heights," Velma says. "I'm not crazy about falling, though."

Velma shuffles across the catwalk toward the green glow. If she can just get closer, she will be able to see what it is.

Just then, she spots something on the ground far below. There are two green glows down there. Now there are three. Now four.

"Jinkies," she says. "What are those things?"

Velma is so curious about the glows below that she forgets about the glow up above. It drifts closer and closer to her.

CREEEEAK.

The catwalk creaks beside Velma and she looks up.

A pale, ghoulish face stares down at her. The figure is dressed as a World War II pilot, with a tattered bomber jacket and flight suit.

Velma's mouth moves but no words come out. Finally, she says, "A g-g-g-ghost pilot!"

Just as the ghost reaches glowing, green hands toward her, Velma turns and runs. She tramps down the catwalk toward the ladder. **CREEEEAK!** The catwalk moans louder. She almost makes it before. . .

SNAP!

Velma plummets as a section of the catwalk snaps beneath her feet. Both she and the piece of metal fall toward the hard floor below. Then, just before she hits, her feet find the piece of catwalk. The metal hits the tail fin of a covered plane and she rides it down like a snowboard.

Velma laughs and holds out her arms to keep balance. "Board grind!"

Turn the page.

Velma rides the metal across the back of the plane and flies off the nose. Pairs of glowing hands reach for her as she sails overhead. She lands on the wing of another plane.

"I need a soft landing," Velma says.

She skids down the wing toward the body of the plane. Then, just before she would slam into it, she spots what she needs. Velma pushes off her metal snowboard, sending it flying. It clatters across the cement floor toward the other end of the hangar. Ghost pilots chase after the noise.

Meanwhile, Velma lands onto a pile of unused tarps. She plows into the soft cushion but tumbles anyway. When she finally comes to a stop, her glasses are gone.

"My glasses," she says. "I can't see a thing without my glasses." Velma crawls across the floor, feeling for her lost glasses.

If Velma finds her glasses, turn to page 44.
If Velma doesn't find her glasses, turn to page 18.

Velma decides to stay on the ground. She crouches behind a covered airplane and watches the green glow move toward the back of the hangar. Velma leaves her hiding spot and follows the glow. As she moves around dusty machinery and more covered planes, she loses sight of the light.

"Now, where did that glow go?" she asks quietly.

She makes her way in the darkness in the direction where she last saw the ghostly light.

"Ouch," she says. She bumps into a long table.

She can't see well in the dim light, but the table is full of strange equipment. There's a stack of papers on one end. She slides a page off the top of the stack.

"This may be a clue," Velma says. She pulls out her flashlight. "I'll have to risk turning on my flashlight to be sure."

She switches on her flashlight and is about to read the page. Then a ghost pilot appears in front of her.

"*Ahhh!*" Velma screams.

The ghost lunges at her. Velma ducks beneath the glowing hands and makes a run for it. She drops her flashlight but still clutches the piece of paper.

Velma tears off across the hangar. Another ghost pilot leaps out from behind an old plane and moves in. Velma leaps into the air as the ghost tries to tackle her.

"I have to get out of here," she says. As Velma runs, she spots an old skateboard up ahead.

Velma leaps into the air and lands atop the skateboard. She kicks the ground with one foot and builds some speed. The chasing ghosts fall behind her.

Turn the page.

"Good riddance," Velma says. She leans left and steers the board toward the window. She'll have to leave the way she came in.

Suddenly, a ghost moves up along her right. Then another ghost moves up along her left. Velma looks down to see that both ghosts are on skateboards, too.

"Jinkies," she says. "Since when do ghosts ride skateboards?"

Each ghost veers toward her. Velma kicks the ground again and pulls ahead. The skateboarding ghosts crisscross behind her.

Velma keeps kicking the ground. But the ghosts keep up with her. She can't lose them.

CREEEEEAK! The hangar doors slowly open.

"Like, good thing Kevin gave us the key to this hangar," Shaggy says. He pushes the door open wider. "Or bad thing if it really is haunted."

"Reah," Scooby agrees. "I don't rike rhosts."

Velma spots the open hangar doors and steers in that direction. "Shaggy! Scooby! Look out!"

"Velma?" Shaggy asks. He squints into the dark hangar. "Is that you?"

Velma doesn't have time to answer. She zips between her friends and out of the hangar.

Shaggy's knees knock together. "Do you see what I see?"

"Reah. Rhosts!" Scooby replies. "Rateboarding Rhosts!"

Before Shaggy and Scooby can get out of the way . . . *BAM!*

"Like, thanks for catching me, Scoobs," says Shaggy. His hands are over his eyes.

"Ruh?" Scooby asks. His big paws cover his own eyes. "I rought you raught me?"

Shaggy and Scooby open their eyes to see where they are. They are each in the arms of a skateboarding ghost pilot.

"Zoinks!" shouts Shaggy. He and Scooby begin to whimper with fear.

Turn the page.

Once outside in the moonlight, Velma looks at the paper in her hand. "Hey," she says. "I think I know what's going on!"

Velma skids to a stop and turns around. She kicks her skateboard and zooms into the hangar. She zips past the ghosts and her frightened friends.

"L-l-like, thanks for the ride, Mr. Ghost," says Shaggy. "But I'd like to get down now?"

Scooby whimpers. "Re too!"

Velma speeds to the back of the hangar and skids to a stop in front of the table full of equipment.

"If my guess is right . . . ," she says as she reaches for a large machine. Velma flicks a switch and smoke billows from one of the machines. A white fog hangs near the hangar's high ceiling.

"Hey, careful with that!" shouts a voice. "That's expensive equipment!"

Turn the page.

The two ghosts carry Scooby and Shaggy over to Velma as she flicks another switch. Another machine comes alive. It projects a ghostly image onto the fog above. It's an image of the phantom plane!

"Rit's the rhost rane," Scooby says.

Scooby scrambles out of the arms of the ghost pilot and climbs atop his glowing head. The ghost loses his balance and the skateboard flies out from under his feet. **BAM!** He crashes to the ground with the big dog piled on top.

"It's all right, Scooby-Doo," says Velma. "It's not a real ghost plane. It's just a projection."

"Then, like, that means the ghosts aren't real, either." Shaggy pulls the rubber mask off one of the ghost pilots. A man's face appears. He sets Shaggy down.

"Then, who are you guys?" asks Shaggy.

"I'm guessing movie promoters," Velma replies.

Velma holds up the piece of paper. It's a flyer advertising a new scary movie called *Ghost Bomber*.

"She's right," grunts the other man. He climbs out from under Scooby and removes his mask. "But we didn't know our special effects would scare everyone away."

"We hoped to spread the word about our movie, then sneak away before anyone found out," says the first man.

"Like, when does the movie come out?" Shaggy asks. "I'd love to see it."

"But you don't like scary movies, Shaggy," Velma says.

Shaggy grins. "No, but I love movie theater popcorn."

"Reah! Ropcorn!" Scooby rubs his belly. "Rooby-rooby-doo!"

THE END

To follow another path, turn to page 17.

Shaggy and Scooby-Doo scramble into the cockpit and climb into the pilot and copilot seats. Scooby puts on a headset and begins pushing buttons.

"Wait a minute, Scoobs," says Shaggy. "Don't touch anything yet."

It's too late. Scooby grabs the control wheel and the plane climbs higher into the sky. With the plane tilted upward, Shaggy flies from his seat. He tumbles back through the body of the plane. He grabs a lever just in time to stop from smacking into the tail of the plane.

"Rorry," Scooby says from the cockpit. The plane levels off.

Shaggy pulls himself forward. Unfortunately, when he pulls on the lever, the bomb bay doors open beneath his feet. "Zoinks!" Shaggy's feet dangle out of the bottom of the plane.

Turn the page.

"Help!" Shaggy yells. "It's about to be bombs away. And, like, that bomb is going to be me!"

Scooby presses more buttons, trying to close the doors. Lights flash, hatches open and close, and static bursts from the radio. He finds controls for everything on the plane but the bomb bay doors.

Suddenly, the plane nose-dives toward the ground.

"What are you doing, Scoobs?" Shaggy asks. He holds on to the lever for dear life.

Scooby shrugs. "Ri don't row!"

The bomber seems to be flying itself. The plane climbs up again and makes a giant loop. The engines roar as it points straight down again. Then, just before it would crash into a million pieces, the bomber levels off once more. The landing gear drops and the plane gently lands on the runway.

When the plane rolls to a stop, Shaggy pries his fingers from the lever. He drops harmlessly out of the hatch, falling a couple of feet to the cement below. Scooby hops out of the plane and joins him. They both breathe a sigh of relief.

Shaggy pats Scooby on the back. "Great flying, pal."

"Uh . . . rank you?" Scooby replies.

"Now, let's find the rest of the gang," Shaggy suggests.

The friends shuffle away from the plane but stop dead in their tracks.

Scooby's teeth chatter. "R-r-r-rhosts, Raggy! Rhosts!"

Shaggy and Scooby-Doo are suddenly surrounded by ghost pilots. Five of the creepy figures move in slowly with outstretched glowing green hands.

"Like, we gotta get outta here," says Shaggy.

If Shaggy and Scooby run to the control tower, turn to page 56.

If Shaggy and Scooby run to the haunted hangar, turn to page 50.

Velma finds her glasses just in time. As she puts them on, an approaching blur turns out to be one of the ghost pilots. She scrambles under a covered airplane to hide. The ghost doesn't see her as it shuffles by.

Keeping to her hiding place, she watches the ghosts search some more. After a while, they gather near a small shed on the other side of the hangar. Velma watches as they go in.

"That sure is a lot of ghosts crammed into a small shed," she says.

Suddenly, the hangar doors slide open. It's Kevin and the rest of the Mystery Inc. gang.

Velma crawls out of her hiding space.

"There you are, Velma," Fred says. "We've been looking everywhere for you. Did you find anything?"

Velma scratches the back of her head. "Well, yes and no."

She tells them about the ghost pilots and how they all disappeared inside the small shed.

Shaggy shivers. "Like, tell me we're not going to go look inside that shed."

"We should definitely go check it out," Velma says.

Shaggy shakes harder. "I told you not to tell me that."

"Reah," Scooby agrees. He dives under a pile of old tarps. Shaggy joins him.

Velma marches over and lifts the tarp. Shaggy and Scooby-Doo cower underneath, whimpering. Velma is about to scold them when she sees what she's holding.

"Hey, guys. I think you found a clue," she says.

"We did?" asks Shaggy.

Velma grips the tarp with both hands and walks backward. The tarp unfurls and she sees that it's not a tarp at all. The cloth is in the shape of an airplane. And not just any airplane. A silver bird is painted on one side, right under painted windows.

Turn the page.

"It's the *Silver Hawk*," says Daphne.

"Why would someone paint a giant piece of cloth to look like a ghost plane?" asks Kevin.

"I don't know," replies Velma. "But I think I know where to look for the answer."

All together, everyone turns to look at the tiny shed on the other side of the hangar.

GULP! Shaggy and Scooby swallow hard.

With Shaggy and Scooby bringing up the rear, Velma leads the way toward the shed. She crouches down and slowly turns the knob. She pulls the door open and peeks inside.

Shaggy covers his eyes. "I can't look."

Scooby does the same. "Me reither!"

Velma swings the door open. The shed is empty. "I don't get it." She walks inside. "All the ghosts came in here."

"And there's only one way in or out," Fred adds.

"Jinkies." Velma steps inside. "Maybe they are real ghosts."

Everyone joins her inside the empty shed.

Shaggy wipes his brow. "I don't know about you, Scoobs." He leans against the wall. "But I'm glad they're gone."

"Reah!" Scooby agrees.

Just then, Shaggy hits a secret button. A square in the wall sinks and a metal door slides over the open shed doorway. Everyone jumps.

"Are we moving?" asks Daphne.

"We sure are," Velma replies. "And we're going down. This shed is really an elevator."

Everyone jumps again as the elevator comes to a stop. The metal door slides open and they are no longer in the hangar. Not the same hangar anyway.

The gang steps out to see a large underground hangar. It's full of soldiers moving crates and strange aircraft.

Turn the page.

"What is this place?" asks Kevin.

"I don't know," Velma replies. "But look."

She points to two familiar figures moving a heavy crate. The men are dressed like the ghost pilots but their faces look normal. One of them spots the kids and drops his end of the crate.

"What are you doing, Reynolds?" asks the other man.

Reynolds fumbles inside the pocket of his tattered bomber jacket. He pulls out a ghost mask and begins putting it on.

Just then, an army general marches toward the gang.

"Keep the mask off, soldiers," the general says. "It's too late. Our cover is blown."

"What's going on here?" Kevin asks the general.

The general shakes his head. "Mr. Ryan, you didn't know it, but when you bought this airfield, it came with a secret. There's a government base underneath what you call the haunted hangar."

"What?" Kevin asks with surprise.

"When we heard you were going to tear down the hangar, we decided we'd better clear out of here," continues the general. "Secretly, of course."

"You've been using the elevator in that old shed?" asks Fred.

The general grins. "There's an even bigger elevator in the hangar floor," he says. "Big enough to move our experimental planes."

"And you covered them with a cloth that made them look like the ghost bomber," Velma adds.

"You guessed it," says the general. "We tried to keep everyone away with those ghost costumes." He shakes his head. "But you kids uncovered our plans before we could make a clean getaway."

"No mystery is too big for Mystery Inc.," Velma says proudly.

THE END

To follow another path, turn to page 17.

Shaggy and Scooby race toward the haunted hangar. With so many creepy ghosts behind them, they don't have time to be scared about what's inside. They are too busy being scared of what's outside. Together, the friends pull open one of the large doors and slip inside. They slide the door behind them.

Shaggy looks around. "This isn't so bad."

Inside, the hangar looks like any other airplane hangar. It's clean, well lit, and full of all kinds of different airplanes.

"Like, I thought this was supposed to be haunted," says Shaggy.

Scooby looks up and gulps. He taps Shaggy's shoulder. "Uh . . . rook up, Raggy."

"Zoinks!" Shaggy jumps when he sees what's above them. High above, up against the roof of the tall hangar is . . . the ghost plane itself!

The ghost plane doesn't look as scary in the lit hangar. It almost doesn't look like a plane at all. It's really a large plane-shaped balloon.

Suddenly, the hangar doors begin to open.

"Come on, Scoobs!" Shaggy leads the way toward the other side of the hangar. They duck into a dark office and shut the door behind them.

"Boy, like, I hope they don't look in here," Shaggy whispers.

"Re, too," Scooby agrees.

The two listen by the door for any signs of the ghosts. Then, they hear a soft moan.

Shaggy gulps. "D-d-did you hear that?"

Then another moan joins the first.

TK·TK·TK·TK·TK·TK·TK·TK! Scooby's teeth chatter. He covers his mouth to keep them quiet.

There's a third moan and then a fourth. The moans aren't coming from outside, with the ghosts. They're coming from inside the room, with Shaggy and Scooby.

Shaggy fumbles around for a light switch.

Turn the page.

When he finds it, he covers his eyes before switching it on. "Like, I really don't want to see if there's a ghost in here."

Shaggy finally switches on the lights and peeks through his fingers. There aren't any ghosts in the room. Instead, it's the rest of the Mystery Inc. gang. Along with Kevin, they're all tied to chairs. Gags cover their mouths. Each of them tries to speak but only a moan can get through the gags.

Shaggy and Scooby untie them. "Like, I'm sure glad there are no ghosts in here after all," Shaggy says.

Velma pulls the gag out of her mouth. "I don't think there are ghosts out there, either."

"Yeah, ghosts don't need to tie people up," Daphne adds.

After everyone is untied, Shaggy looks around the room. It's full of worktables with electronic equipment. RC controllers are scattered about. They are the kind of remotes used to control toy planes, cars, and helicopters.

"What's with all the radio controllers?" asks Shaggy.

"They're not mine," says Kevin. "But I think I know whose they are."

Fred picks up one of the controllers and extends the antenna. "Before you tell us, let's catch some ghosts!" He hands everyone a controller.

Outside, the ghost pilots creep through the hangar. They close in on the office in the back. Suddenly, the office door bursts open and Kevin and the Mystery Inc. gang proudly step out. Each of them wields an RC controller.

"Hit it," says Fred.

They all flip switches on their controllers. The airplanes around them roar to life. The planes begin to chase the ghosts around the hangar. The once-scary ghosts are scared themselves as they run from radio-controlled planes.

Turn the page.

The ghost pilots make a break for the hangar doors. Before they escape, Kevin steps out with a controller of his own. He works the joystick and the *Silver Hawk* rolls into view. It blocks the ghosts' escape. Beaten, the ghoulish pilots turn around and raise their hands above their heads.

Kevin steps forward. "Steve? Are you in there?"

One of the pilots steps forward and removes his mask. It's a bearded man with black hair.

"Who's that?" asks Fred.

"My ex-business partner, Steve Kavner," Kevin explains. "Steve wanted to create a completely radio-controlled air show." Kevin holds up the controller. "I thought this looked like your work."

"It'll work, I tell ya," Kavner barks.

"I told you then and I'm saying it now," says Kevin. "It's not safe."

"It's also not safe to try to fool Mystery Inc.," Fred adds.

THE END

To follow another path, turn to page 17

Shaggy and Scooby take off toward the airfield's control tower. The ghoulish ghost pilots are right behind them, closing in fast. When the friends reach the tower, they fling open the door. Shaggy and Scooby duck inside and lock the door behind them. The ghosts pound on the locked door.

"Raggy, rook!" says Scooby. He holds up his paws. They glow green in the darkened room.

"Your paws are glowing just like the ghosts," says Shaggy. "Maybe you picked up something from the airplane's controls."

"A rue!" says Scooby.

"You're right, buddy," Shaggy agrees. "That is a clue!"

The door buckles behind them.

"Come on, Scoobs." Shaggy runs up the stairs toward the tower. "Like, that door won't hold for long."

The two friends race up winding stairs to the tower. They burst open the door and slam it shut behind them.

In a whirlwind, Shaggy and Scooby move desks, chairs, and lamps in front of the door, creating a barricade.

Shaggy slaps his hands together. "That should hold them."

There are large windows on all four walls of the control tower. They can see the entire airfield in all directions. The moonlight gives the place an especially creepy look.

"Hey, Scoobs. Look at this." Shaggy picks up an RC controller. It is the kind used to pilot radio-controlled model planes. Shaggy flips a switch and, way down on the runway, the bomber's engines roar to life.

"Someone was controlling the bomber the entire time," Shaggy says.

Scooby nods in agreement.

BAM! Something slams against the control tower door. The entire barricade shakes.

"Like, that's not going to hold them after all," says Shaggy.

Turn the page.

BAM! BAM! The door shakes again. A lamp tumbles from the pile and smashes on the ground.

Shaggy's lower lip trembles. He holds out a hand to Scooby. "Like, it's been nice knowing you, pal."

Scooby gives him a paw and shakes. "Rou too, Raggy."

Just before tears fill Shaggy's eyes, he spots something outside the window. It's a rope.

Shaggy's eyes widen. "Come on, Scoobs!" Shaggy opens the window and grabs the rope. "Let's climb out of here."

"Rokay!" replies Scooby-Doo.

Shaggy and Scooby climb out of the tower window just as the ghosts break through the barricade. The friends plan to climb down to the ground but the rope moves away from the tower.

Shaggy looks up to see the rope attached to the ghost bomber itself. "Zoinks! It's the ghost plane!"

Turn to page 91.

Fred and Daphne hop down from the wing tip. There are no other old planes in sight, but they keep running. In the moonlight, they see that they are in a large open field.

"Where are we?" asks Daphne.

"I think we're on the other side of the airplane graveyard," replies Fred.

"You mean we have to go back through the graveyard to find the others?" asks Daphne.

"Or walk all the way around," says Fred. "At least we lost those ghosts. They'll never be able to spot us out here in the dark."

Suddenly lights switch on all around them. They can see each other clearly, as if it were daytime. The bright lights form two rows, stretching across the open field.

"What's with the lights?" Daphne asks.

"They look like runway lights," Fred says.

Daphne shakes her head. "But the airfield is on the other side of the airplane graveyard."

"Look out!" Fred shouts.

He grabs Daphne's hand and dives to the side. They fly over the row of lights and tumble to the ground. They narrowly miss being squashed by a landing plane, a very large and quiet plane.

Daphne points at the plane. "Look familiar?"

As the plane pulls to a stop, the lights shine on the plane's body. A large silver hawk emblem is painted on the plane's nose.

Fred gasps. "It's the ghost plane!"

Daphne gulps. "Up close and personal."

"Too close." Fred looks around. "You think we should hide somewhere?"

"I don't know." Daphne raises an eyebrow. "Maybe we should take a closer look."

To get a closer look at the ghost plane, turn to page **79**.
To find a hiding spot and keep watch, turn to page **96**.

Velma makes her way across the now-empty airfield toward the haunted hangar. "I don't know if the hangar has something to do with that ghost plane," she says to herself. "But with a name like 'haunted hangar', a good detective should check it out."

Velma strolls up to the large main doors and jerks the handle. Neither door will budge.

"It can never be easy, can it?" she mutters. "There must be another way inside this place."

She moves around the hangar until she spots a small window. She gives the window a try. It's unlocked!

Velma crawls through the window and looks around. The hangar has a huge floor plan with a rounded roof high above. No lights are on but many windows let in shafts of pale moonlight. Old planes and large pieces of equipment are covered with dusty tarps.

Velma pulls out her flashlight but doesn't switch it on. If there is anyone in there with her, she doesn't want them to see her.

"Kinda creepy," she whispers. "But not enough to call it haunted."

Velma changes her mind when she spies an eerie green glow on the other side of the hangar. It floats around various pieces of covered equipment.

"Jinkies," she whispers. "That makes things a little creepier."

Then she spots another green glow. This one floats among the catwalks high above. The catwalks are long, narrow walkways that crisscross near the high ceiling.

"Decisions, decisions," she whispers.

If Velma climbs up to the catwalks, turn to page 28.
If Velma stays on the ground, turn to page 32.

Daphne and Fred take off down the row of planes. With the ghost in pursuit, they sprint back the way they came, toward the main airfield.

As they are about to leave the airplane graveyard, they are cut off. Two more ghostly airmen appear in front of them. They also wear tattered flight suits, and one wears a ragged leather jacket. They both have the same glowing hands and faces.

"Jeepers!" Daphne skids to a stop. "We're cut off!"

Fred scrambles onto the wing of an airplane. "This way," he says. He reaches down and pulls up Daphne.

The two run atop the large airplane to make their escape. Unfortunately, the ghosts climb up after them. Fred and Daphne jump onto the body of the plane and hop down onto the other wing. They keep running until they reach the end of that wing.

"We're going to have to jump for it," says Daphne.

Daphne sprints ahead and vaults off the end of the wing tip. She somersaults in midair and lands on the wing tip of the next plane over.

"I'm not a gymnast," says Fred. He jumps off the wing tip with both feet. "But I can still make it." He lands on the other wing next to Daphne.

She smiles. "But without as much style."

Fred and Daphne dart up the wing, toward that plane's body. The three ghosts jump across and continue the chase.

Leaping from one wing tip to another, Fred and Daphne run across the tops of several planes in the graveyard. They put plenty of distance between themselves and the ghost pilots. Unfortunately, they reach the end of the wing and the end of the airplane graveyard.

"Let's hop down and make a break for it," Fred suggests.

"I think we should find some place to hide," Daphne counters.

To follow Fred's suggestion, turn to page 60.
To go with Daphne's idea, turn to page 76.

Daphne beats her fists on the ghost pilot's back. "Put me down right now!" she orders. The ghost ignores her and continues hauling her over his shoulder. They move through the inside of a large empty airplane.

"Guess I'll have to do it myself," Daphne says.

She reaches up and grabs a metal bar on the ceiling. She grips tight and jerks herself free from the fiend's grasp. Daphne tucks in her legs and performs a midair somersault. She gracefully lands behind the shocked ghost.

"Sorry, gotta run!" Daphne takes off down the long plane's body.

As she runs, Daphne looks for a way out. But when she reaches the end of the plane, another long corridor stretches out before her. Two of the planes are connected somehow. She darts through the second plane's body. She soon finds another passageway jutting off in another direction.

Turn the page.

"Someone connected a bunch of these old planes together," she says to herself.

Daphne runs some more until she finds three corridors splitting off in different directions.

"I have to find a way out of this maze," she says. "But first I have to lose that pesky ghost."

Daphne turns down one of the corridors and crouches in the shadows. She isn't there long before her pursuing ghost appears. He stops and glances down each of the passages. Lucky for Daphne, he chooses one of the other corridors. He runs away from her and out of sight.

Daphne stands and walks down the dark passage. She turns another corner and then spots something up ahead.

"I think I see light," she says.

Daphne makes her way toward the light. The corridor ends in a wide opening. The end of the airplane is completely gone. Daphne reaches the opening and peers out. She can't believe what she sees.

Turn to page 72.

After everyone splits up, Shaggy turns to Scooby-Doo. "I don't know about you, pal. But, like, I don't want any part of an airplane graveyard or a haunted hangar."

Scooby crosses his arms and shakes his head. "Uh-uh! Me reither!"

"Like, let's go see if Kevin found out what's wrong with his bomber," Shaggy says.

"Rokay," agrees Scooby-Doo.

Shaggy and Scooby shuffle out onto the airstrip and find Kevin talking to the flight crew of his replica bomber.

"I don't know, Mr. Ryan," says one of the pilots to him. "The number-three engine blew and the rest just shut down."

Just then, Scooby-Doo spots an eerie green glow. It's coming from inside the plane, through the bomber's main hatch. The dog's knees begin to quiver. He taps Shaggy on the shoulder.

"Just a second, buddy," Shaggy says. He's busy listening to Kevin and the others.

Turn the page.

Scooby sees a spooky figure emerge from the hatch. The figure wears a tattered flight suit and faded leather bomber jacket. Its glowing green face has two hollow eyes and a wide mouth.

"A rho . . . ," Scooby tries to say. He shivers all over. "A r-r-rho. . ."

"What's that, Scoobs?" asks Shaggy.

Scooby-Doo springs into Shaggy's arms. "A rhost! A rhost!"

The ghost pilot leaps from the plane and lunges for Kevin and the others. The people scatter as the ghost moves in.

"Come on, Scoobs," says Shaggy. "Hide!"

Shaggy and Scooby-Doo run to the back of the airplane. Shaggy pulls open a small hatch in the tail of the plane. He and Scooby scramble inside and close the metal door behind them.

"I think we'll be safe here," Shaggy whispers.

"Reah! Reah!" Scooby-Doo agrees.

Just then, the plane begins to vibrate.

"Like, I don't feel so safe anymore," Shaggy says.

Shaggy carefully opens the hatch and peers outside. To their shock, they see the ground falling away from them. The airfield looks very tiny now. They're flying!

Shaggy closes the hatch and swallows hard. "Come on, Scoobs. Let's see how bad this is."

Shaggy and Scooby make their way to the front of the bomber. When they reach the cockpit, they see that no one is flying the plane.

"Okay. It's really bad," says Shaggy. "Have you ever flown a plane, Scoobs?"

"Ronly in rideogames," replies Scooby-Doo.

Scooby-Doo looks around and spots a parachute pack hanging inside the plane. "Rook, Raggy! Rook!"

"Oh, no," says Shaggy. "Like, there's only one parachute and two of us."

If Shaggy and Scooby try to fly the plane, turn to page 40.

If Shaggy and Scooby share a parachute, turn to page 82.

It turns out that Daphne is inside an old airplane body poking out of a huge pile of junk.

"Wow. This is more than an airplane graveyard," she says to herself. "This is an airplane scrapyard."

She looks around to see that there are other junk piles nearby. In fact, the heaps of old airplanes and airplane parts surround a giant pit in the ground. The crater is lit brightly by several work lights. A tall crane holds a small platform on the edge of the large pit.

"What's going on here?" Daphne asks. There are figures down beside the pit, but Daphne can't make out who they are. "If I'm going to find out, I need to get closer."

Daphne carefully climbs out of the plane and onto the junk pile. Careful not to cause an airplane-part landslide, she makes her way down the mountain of junk. When she nears the crane, Daphne can make out who it is.

"That's the documentary filmmaker Sheila Wilcox," Daphne whispers. "And she's talking to one of the ghosts."

Daphne is still too far away to hear what they are saying. She climbs down some more. Then she slinks into the cab of the large crane. Now she can see and hear what they are saying. That's when the other two ghosts appear. They join Wilcox on the crane's platform.

"We lost them," one of the ghosts says. Then he reaches up and pulls off his mask.

"Why, he's not a ghost at all," Daphne whispers.

"Well, you better find them," barks Sheila Wilcox.

Daphne has an idea. She reaches down and moves one of the crane's control levers. **RRRRRRRRRUMBLE!** The crane roars to life. The main cable tightens and the platform begins to rise.

Turn to page 94.

Velma lifts the tarp. "Quick. Hide under here."

The three hide beneath the tarp as the ghosts close in. They can see five green glows on the other side of the thin tarp. Then they hear something they can't believe. The ghosts speak!

"You think we scared them off?" asks one voice.

"I hope so," replies another. "We have to finish this plane before tomorrow."

Velma doesn't recognize the voice. But then she hears a voice she does recognize.

"Hello? Like, anyone in here?" It is Shaggy.

"There's another one," says one of the ghosts. "Let's get him."

"No, we'll get you!" Velma shouts. Velma, Daphne, and Fred rip the tarp off the plane and throw it over the struggling ghost pilots.

"What's going on?" asks Shaggy as he and Scooby run into view.

"We just solved the mystery," Velma announces. "That's what."

Velma reaches down and uncovers one of the ghost pilots. She pulls the mask from his head.

"That's Dirk Wilson," gasps Daphne. "He raced against Kevin."

Velma rubs a smudge of black paint from the plane. "And I bet this plane is red underneath this fresh coat of paint."

"You mean, like, that's Kevin's plane?" asks Shaggy.

Dirk lowers his head. "Yeah, I'm sick of always getting beaten by Kevin," Dirk admits. "I had that ghost bomber painted on the bottom of one of the blimps as a distraction. I thought if I traded planes with Kevin, I could win for once."

"Like, what good is winning if you cheat?" asks Shaggy.

Velma crosses her arms. "That's why Mystery Incorporated never cheats when it comes to solving mysteries!"

THE END

To follow another path, turn to page 17.

Daphne kneels and spots a small hatch on the top of the plane. "In here," she says, opening the hatch and dropping inside.

Fred follows and closes the door behind him. They stand in darkness while footsteps clomp overhead. After things quiet down, Daphne risks switching on the flashlight.

They are inside a very large airplane. But it's a very strange airplane. Except for a single pilot's seat, it's completely hollow.

"What a strange plane," says Fred.

Daphne reaches out and touches the side. She runs her hand over its smooth surface and then knocks quietly. **TONK. TONK.** "It's made of plastic."

Fred and Daphne wait a bit longer to make sure the coast is clear. Then they move toward the side hatch. Fred carefully opens it and slowly peeks outside.

"I don't see anything." Fred opens it all the way and hops out.

Daphne follows him. She quietly shuts the hatch behind her. Then she moves the flashlight beam up and across the plane. "Fred, look."

The beam lands on an image of a large silver bird. They back away as she lights up the rest of the plane. It is painted to look old and decaying. But they had been inside the thing and knew that wasn't true.

"It's the ghost bomber," she says. "Here's where it ended up."

"Hollow and plastic," Fred says. "The bomber is really a glider. That's why it didn't make a sound when it flew over us."

Daphne switches off her flashlight. "We'd better get back to the others to tell them what we found."

Turn the page.

Fred leads the way as they creep back between rows of old planes. After reaching the end of the long plane, he stops.

"Hang on," Fred says. "Let me see if there are any more of those ghost pilots."

Fred leans out and checks for ghosts. While he searches, a hatch silently opens in the plane beside them. A ghost pilot reaches out and covers Daphne's mouth with a glowing green hand.

"We can't be too careful," Fred adds. "Those ghosts can be anywhere."

The ghost wraps his other arm around Daphne and pulls her into the plane. The hatch closes just as quietly.

"I don't see anyone," Fred reports. "Come on."

Fred moves farther down the row of planes. He thinks Daphne is still behind him.

To follow Fred, turn to page 86.
To follow Daphne, turn to page 67.

Fred and Daphne chase after the ghost bomber as it pulls to the end of the secret runway. As it nears the edge of the airplane graveyard, they duck behind a small junk pile.

"Look," Fred whispers.

The main hatch opens and a ghost pilot steps out. He marches away from the bomber toward the body of a wrecked airplane. He opens the hatch on the old plane and steps inside. A dim glow comes from the entryway.

"Let's get a closer look," Daphne suggests.

Fred and Daphne sneak over to the wrecked plane and peer inside the open hatch. There are four ghost pilots inside. They stand in front of a man sitting at a desk.

Turn the page.

"I thought I told you not to fly so low over the crowd," says the man at the desk. "You scared everyone away. And now I have those blasted kids from Mystery Inc. snooping all over the place."

"Sorry, boss," says the ghost. "But the new plane flies great. And it doesn't make a sound."

"Good, good," says the man. "With all the parts in Ryan's airplane graveyard, we'll be able to build five more, easy."

"And sell them for big bucks," says the ghost. Only he's not a ghost after all. He and the other ghost have their masks pulled up, revealing their faces.

"Aren't those some of the guys from Dan's work crew?" asks Daphne.

"That's right," Fred whispers. "And you know who the boss must be."

Fred steps into the doorway. "I don't think Kevin will appreciate you stealing his airplane parts."

Daphne leans in. "Isn't that right, Mechanic Dan?"

Dan stands up from behind the desk. "It's those kids!" he shouts. "Get 'em!"

Fred and Daphne step out of the plane and slam the hatch shut. Fred grabs a nearby propeller blade and slides it through the handle. Mechanic Dan and all his phony ghosts are trapped inside the wrecked plane.

"Hey!" shouts Dan. "You can't lock us in here!"

"Don't worry," says Daphne. "Once we round up the rest of the gang, I'm sure Kevin will let you out."

"Yeah," Fred agrees. "Once the police get here, of course. They just love hearing from us at Mystery Inc."

THE END

To follow another path, turn to page 17.

Shaggy straps on the parachute pack. Once the straps are pulled tight, he and Scooby shuffle toward the main hatch. Shaggy looks down at the tiny airfield below. His face turns green and his knees knock together. *TOK·TOK·TOK·TOK·TOK·TOK!*

"Like, maybe there's a third choice we can make," says Shaggy. "Whadya think, buddy?"

Scooby shakes his head. "Uh-uh. Rook!"

Suddenly, the ghost pilot appears inside the plane. It reaches for them with glowing, green hands.

"Zoinks!" Shaggy shouts.

Scooby jumps into Shaggy's arms and Shaggy jumps through the open hatch. They fall out of the plane and tumble down, down, down. The tiny airfield grows larger and larger below them.

"Pull the cord!" Shaggy shouts. "Like, pull the cord!"

Scooby searches the parachute pack for the rip cord. He spots a handle and pulls it. A large red parachute billows from the pack. It catches air, and Shaggy and Scooby float slowly downward.

Shaggy looks around and enjoys the view. "This isn't so bad."

Scooby's eyes widen. "It's rad! It's rad!"

The bomber circles around and flies straight at them. Shaggy tries to run away, but his legs just kick in the air. The bomber buzzes the parachute, sending Shaggy and Scooby flipping over and over and over again.

"Whoa-whoa-whoa-whoa!" shout Shaggy and Scooby.

When they finally stop spinning, the parachute floats them toward the woods near the airfield. Below them, they spot the bomber going in for a landing. Shaggy and Scooby land in the middle of a huge tree. The parachute snags on the upper branches and they dangle from the top of the tall tree.

Turn the page.

"Like, we're trapped, Scoobs," says Shaggy.

Scooby looks over the belts on Shaggy's parachute pack. He spots a button in the middle of a large buckle. Scooby pushes the button and the straps fall away. So do Shaggy and Scooby. They plummet toward the ground below. Luckily, the many tree branches slow their fall.

"Ooh! Ow! Ooh! Ah! Ooh! Ouch!" they shout as they hit each branch.

BAM! Shaggy and Scooby finally land in a clump of bushes. They poke their heads out of the leaves. Twigs poke out of their hair. Their eyes spin and they hear chirping birds.

"Like, we should get back and warn the others," says Shaggy. He rubs his head. "But I must've hit my head really hard. I smell something delicious."

If Shaggy and Scooby return to the airfield, turn to page 99.

If Shaggy and Scooby investigate the food smell, turn to page 20.

Fred tiptoes as he moves silently beside the next plane. When he reaches the end, he holds a hand up behind him. "Hang on. Let me check again."

As Fred scans the area, another hatch opens behind him. Another ghost appears and steps out of the plane.

"Coast is clear," Fred whispers. "Let's go."

This time, as Fred tiptoes out from behind the plane, the ghost tiptoes after him. Fred keeps an eye out for ghosts, but he doesn't know one is right behind him.

"Do you see anything?" Fred whispers, thinking he's talking to Daphne.

"*Mmmmmmm*," moans the ghost.

"What was that?" Fred asks without turning around.

"*Mmmmmmm*," the ghost repeats.

"I can't understand you if you mumble like that," Fred says as he turns around.

Fred spots the ghost and his eyes widen. "Whoa!" He jumps high into the air. His legs are already running before he hits the ground again.

The ghost lunges for him but Fred is already out of there. He tears through the airplane graveyard. Fred pours on the speed but the ghost is close behind.

"This is one fast ghost," Fred says. "I need a place to hide."

Fred dives underneath one of the large planes. He scrambles to the other side and spots a perfect hiding spot. It's an open cockpit of a smaller plane. Fred climbs into the cockpit and ducks down. He hears the ghost run past.

"What happened to Daphne?" he asks. "I have to get out of here and find her."

Fred begins to climb out but is slammed back into the cockpit as the plane begins to move. "I hope this thing isn't taking off," Fred says. "I don't know how to fly a plane."

Turn the page.

Fred pops his head out and looks around. To his relief, Fred sees that the plane isn't taking off—it's being towed by a large truck. Unfortunately, the truck hauls him and the plane out of the airplane graveyard, toward the airfield.

"How am I going to find Daphne, now?" he asks.

Fred is about to jump out of the cockpit when he freezes. Three ghost pilots run after the plane. They stare at him with dark eyes and reach for him with glowing hands.

"If I hop out now, those ghosts will nab me for sure," says Fred.

As the truck pulls the plane onto the runway, bright lights flash over them. Another vehicle drives toward them on the airfield. And it's not just any vehicle.

"The Mystery Machine!" Fred shouts.

The truck pulls to a stop on the runway. Meanwhile, the Mystery Machine swings around and cuts off the ghosts' escape.

Kevin, Velma, Shaggy, and Scooby pile out of the van.

Fred waves at them. "Hey, gang!"

"What are you doing in my plane?" asks Kevin.

Fred leans out of the cockpit and looks at the plane. Sure enough, it's Kevin's race plane.

The truck door opens and, to Fred's surprise, Daphne hops out. "I think I can answer that," she says.

Fred climbs out of the plane and joins her beside the ghost pilots.

"After I got away from one of the ghosts, I spotted your plane hooked up to this truck," she explained. "I knew someone was trying to steal it. And when I saw Fred climb inside, I decided to steal it back."

Turn the page.

"Who would want to steal my plane?" asks Kevin.

Fred juts a thumb at the three ghosts. "Why don't you ask them?"

The three ghosts shuffle nervously, their heads down. The one in the middle reaches up and pulls off a mask.

Kevin recognizes him at once. "Rocket Rodney?"

"Like, the stunt pilot?" asks Shaggy.

"That's right," says Rodney. "Your plane is so fast, I wanted it for my stunt team." He snarls at Daphne and Fred. "I almost got away with it, too. If it weren't for you meddling kids."

Daphne smiles. "Another win for Mystery Inc."

THE END

To follow another path, turn to page 17.

The ghost plane doesn't act like a plane at all. It drifts sideways away from the tower. Shaggy and Scooby hold tight to the rope as they float toward the runway.

"It's a ralloon!" shouts Scooby-Doo. The two of them dangle beneath a giant plane-shaped balloon.

"I'm glad it's not a ghost plane," says Shaggy. "But how are we going to get down?"

Scooby spots a pair of headlights heading their way. "Rook!" A small white van pulls onto the runway.

"Yay!" shouts Shaggy. "The Mystery Machine!"

"And some rhosts," adds Scooby-Doo.

As the Mystery Machine drives toward them, the ghost pilots pour out of the control tower. They run across the airfield, after the van.

Fred pokes his head out of the driver's window. "Hold on, guys!"

The van pulls beneath the dangling duo. Shaggy lets go first, landing on the roof.

Turn the page.

"Your turn, Scoobs!" Shaggy shouts.

Scooby is about to let go when he hears a noise from above. **RRRRRIP!** The rope tears a big hole in the side of the balloon plane. Scooby finally drops to the roof, and the van rolls to a stop.

The deflating plane flops down behind the van. It covers the chasing ghost pilots. They try to fight their way out, but it's no use.

Fred, Velma, Daphne, and Kevin climb out of the van. Scooby and Shaggy scramble down off the roof. They gather around the many lumps struggling under the deflated balloon.

"Looks as if you caught some ghosts," says Velma.

"Scooby caught the ghosts," Shaggy admits. "With the ghost plane itself."

One of the floundering figures pokes his head out from under the balloon. "Get this thing off me. I can't breathe."

Everyone thinks he is talking about the balloon but he really means his mask. The ghost reaches up and pulls off his mask. Underneath, it is . . .

"Dan," says Kevin.

"Your mechanic?" asks Daphne.

"That's him," replies Kevin. "What's the big idea, Dan?"

"Ah, I wanted to sell the *Silver Hawk*," Dan grumbles. He looks up at the Mystery Inc. gang. "Kevin wanted to donate it to a museum." He shakes his head. "All that hard work and he doesn't even want to make a buck. I would've made lots of bucks . . . if it wasn't for you meddling kids."

"It wasn't meddling kids," says Kevin. "Sounds as if it was a meddling dog."

Scooby wags his tail and giggles. "Rooby-Rooby-Doo!"

THE END

To follow another path, turn to page 17.

Sheila Wilcox and her three henchmen jump as they are lifted high into the air. Daphne moves another lever and the platform swings closer to the crane's cab.

"Put us down this instant!" Wilcox demands.

"No way," shouts Daphne. "Not until you tell me what you're up to."

Wilcox sighs. "My last documentary was about treasure hunters," she explains. "I tried to tell Kevin that there may be buried treasure here, but he wouldn't listen. So I decided to scare everyone away with that phony ghost plane and look for it myself. Now put us down!"

"Hmm, maybe after I get Kevin and the rest of Mystery Inc.," Daphne says. "And don't forget the authorities, of course."

Wilcox waves her fist. "You can't do this!"

Daphne smiles. "Sure we can. We're Mystery Inc."

THE END

To follow another path, turn to page 17.

"There!" Fred points to a small shack.

They run across the field, and Fred flings open the door. They duck inside and close the door. Fred peeks out of a small window on the door.

Daphne pulls out her flashlight and switches it on. Her blood turns cold when she spots what's in the shack with them. Two ghost pilots stare down at her with hollow black eyes.

"Fr-Fr-Fr-Fred?" Daphne stammers.

"Hang on a second," Fred whispers. "I want to see who gets out of the plane."

Daphne taps on Fred's shoulder with a trembling hand. "Fr-Fr-Fr-Fred." Her flashlight trembles in her other hand.

"Keep that light still, will ya?" says Fred. "Someone might see it."

Finally, Daphne grabs Fred's shoulder and spins him around. "Fred! Look!"

Fred's eyes widen. "Yikes!"

Fred spins back around and flings open the door. Fred and Daphne try to bolt from the shack at the same time. They get stuck shoulder-to-shoulder in the door jam. Both pairs of legs run in midair. They go nowhere fast!

Fred finally stops running. "Hey. Why haven't they nabbed us yet?"

After a few more strides, Daphne stops, too. "Yeah. We should be toast by now."

Fred and Daphne carefully unjam themselves. They turn back and examine the two ghosts. Fred leans in for a closer look.

"These aren't ghosts at all," he says. He picks up one of the floppy arms. "These are just old flight suits with ghost masks."

"So that means the other ghosts aren't real either," Daphne says.

Fred smiles. "And I think we just found a way to get a closer look at that ghost plane."

Turn the page.

A couple of minutes later, Fred and Daphne are dressed as ghost pilots. They march across the field toward the old bomber. It's parked just beside the airplane graveyard. The plane's hatch is open but there's no movement in or around the plane. Fred and Daphne move closer.

Then, just as they are about to close in, they stop cold.

"Do you see that?" Fred asks beneath his mask.

"I sure do," replies Daphne.

Up ahead, ghost pilots emerge from the airplane graveyard. But they aren't alone. Each ghost has a prisoner walking in front of him. The prisoners are Kevin and the rest of the Mystery Inc. gang. The ghosts march them into the waiting ghost plane. Everyone disappears inside.

"They caught all our friends," whispers Fred. "We have to rescue them somehow."

Turn to page 102.

Shaggy and Scooby run through the woods toward the airfield. They're almost through the trees when . . . **_KLANGGG!_** They slam into a long metal bar. Their feet keep running but they no longer touch the ground.

"Ruh-roh," says Scooby-Doo.

"Oh boy, Scoobs," says Shaggy. "Like, here we go again."

They hold onto the bar and find themselves soaring high into the air. They shiver with fear and grip the bar even tighter.

Scooby glances up. "Rook, Raggy!"

Shaggy looks up to see that they are flying a giant hang-glider. It's not just any hang-glider. The huge glider is painted to look like the spooky ghost plane.

"The *Rilver Rawk*!" Scooby says.

"Like, the ghost plane isn't real," says Shaggy. "And if that isn't real, I'll bet the ghost isn't either."

Below them, they spot the ghost pilot near Kevin Ryan's replica bomber.

Turn the page.

"You think we can steer this thing, Scoobs?" Shaggy asks.

Scooby-Doo nods. "Reah! Reah!" His long tongue flaps in the breeze.

Shaggy grins. "Then let's do it, pal!"

Together, Shaggy and Scooby lean to the left, then to the right. Pretty soon, they steer the glider toward the ghost pilot below. The pilot spots the incoming hang-glider and tries to escape. Shaggy and Scooby chase him out onto the runway.

The ghost runs like crazy but it's no use. Soon, Shaggy and Scooby are right above him.

"Rook out berow!" Scooby shouts.

FLAM! The hang-glider crumples atop the spooky pilot. Shaggy, Scooby, and the pilot are tangled in a web of painted cloth and thin cables.

"Like, who turned out the lights?!" Shaggy asks.

The Mystery Machine pulls to a stop in front of them. The van's headlights light the scene as Kevin and the rest of the gang climb out.

"What's that?" asks Fred.

"That's the ghost plane," Shaggy replies, climbing out of the wrecked glider. He points to a head poking out of the shambles. "And that's the ghost."

Shaggy pulls the ghost mask off the man's head.

"Wait, I know him," says Kevin. "That's Stanley Shafer. He's building his own replica of the *Silver Hawk*."

"I didn't want you to fly yours before I got mine off the ground," Shafer growls. "I just needed to buy a little more time." He shakes his head. "And I would've gotten away with it, too, if it weren't for you meddling kids."

"Like, it's going to be even harder to fly your plane from jail," says Shaggy.

"Reah!" agrees Scooby-Doo.

THE END

To follow another path, turn to page 17.

Daphne taps her chin. "Say, what if we need just one ghost to get inside?"

"What do you mean?" asks Fred.

Daphne reaches over and removes Fred's ghost mask. "That's how we get in," she says. "I'll bring in another prisoner."

Fred grins. "Great idea." He pulls off the tattered flight suit. With his normal clothes beneath, he soon looks the same as always.

Dressed as a ghost, Daphne marches him over to the plane. They reach the open hatch and pause. No sound comes from inside. Fred takes a deep breath and steps inside.

Once inside, Fred and Daphne see all of their friends. The group sits quietly around a long table. They look up at Fred with scared expressions. A ghost pilot stands behind each one. Kevin sits at the head of the table.

Daphne shoves Fred forward. "I caught another one," she says in a deep voice.

"Good," says Kevin. He stands and points to the other end of the long table. "Sit him there."

Daphne pretends to force Fred into the chair.

"Kevin? You're behind all this?" asks Fred.

Kevin laughs. "Of course. With a ghost plane, an airplane graveyard, and a haunted hangar . . . I knew that Mystery Inc. couldn't resist."

Fred can't believe his ears. Kevin was supposed to be their friend.

"But why?" asks Fred. "Why did you want to get us here?"

Kevin smiles. "Oh, I needed you all here for one very important reason . . ."

"SURPRISE!" everyone shouts.

Suddenly his friends are all smiling and laughing. Everyone produces party hats and puts them on. Daphne pulls off her mask and places a hat on top of Fred's head.

Shaggy blows a party whistle. "Like, happy birthday, Fred."

Turn the page.

"A surprise party?!" Fred asks.

The ghost pilots set out plates, silverware, and best of all, a big birthday cake. The cake has the shape of the ghost plane on top.

"I can't believe you went to so much trouble," says Fred.

"What better kind of party for a Mystery Inc. member than a mystery party?" asks Velma.

"Roh, boy!" Scooby licks his lips with his long tongue. "Rirthday Rake!"

"Now, Scooby," says Daphne. "Make sure Fred gets some before you eat it all."

Scooby's ears droop. "Rokay."

"Yeah, buddy," Shaggy agrees. "Like, it won't be a mystery if this plane disappears."

THE END

To follow another path, turn to page 17.

AUTHOR

Michael Anthony Steele has written for television shows such as *Wishbone* and *Barney & Friends* and has authored just over 100 books for various characters and brands, including: Batman, Green Lantern, Shrek, LEGO City, Spider-Man, Tony Hawk, Word Girl, Garfield, Night at the Museum and The Penguins of Madagascar. Ant lives in Texas but travels all over the country visiting schools and libraries.

ILLUSTRATOR

Scott Neely has been a professional illustrator and designer for many years. Since 1999, he's been an official Scooby-Doo and Cartoon Network artist, working on such licensed properties as Dexter's Laboratory, Johnny Bravo, Courage The Cowardly Dog, Powerpuff Girls and more. He has also worked on Pokémon, Mickey Mouse Clubhouse, My Friends Tigger & Pooh, Handy Manny, Strawberry Shortcake, Bratz and many other popular characters. He lives in a suburb of Philadelphia.

GLOSSARY

airfield (air-FEELD)—large section of land set aside for the takeoff, landing, and repair of aircraft

bleachers (BLEE-churz)—rows of long benches for spectators

blimp (BLIMP)—inflatable airship full of helium with an attached cabin for the pilot, crew, and passengers

catwalk (CAT-wawk)—thin walkway or bridge, usually high above the floor

hangar (HANG-ur)—large, wide building with a high roof; used for storing aircraft

hatch (HACH)—door on an airplane, ship, or submarine

pylon (PIE-lon)—tower or post used to mark a flight path for an airplane

RC (ar-see)—short for radio controlled; directing a remote device like a toy plane or car with radio waves

runway (RUHN-way)—long strip of smooth ground that airplanes use for takeoff and landing

skewer (SKYOO-ur)—long piece of wood or metal used for cooking food over a fire

tarpaulin (TAR-puh-lin)—heavy-duty cloth or plastic sheet for protecting things from water or dust; tarp for short

taxi (TAK-see)—when an airplane rolls slowly across the ground before taking off

YOU CHOOSE JOKES!

YOU CHOOSE which punch line is funniest!

How can a ghost pilot fly a plane?
a. **He wings it.**
b. **Eerie-plane training.**
c. **He's good at terror-flying.**

How does Shaggy like his pizza at the air show?
a. **Plane.**
b. **Jumbo jet size.**
c. **With extra propelleroni.**

What was the spookiest thing Scooby
saw at the air show?
a. **A horror-copter.**
b. **A flying sorcerer.**
c. **An empty concession stand.**

Who did the ghost pilot take to the air show?
a. His ghoul friend.
b. A fright attendant.
c. Another spooktator.

What did Velma say to the ghost pilot?
a. "Straighten up and fly right!"
b. "Your job is up in the air!"
c. "You really took off at the beginning,
   but now you're going to bomb!"

Why was the ghost pilot angry
at the dry cleaners?
a. They didn't let his scarf
   scare dry.
b. They repaired the tear in
   his leather jacket.
c. They put his flight suit
   on the wrong hangar.

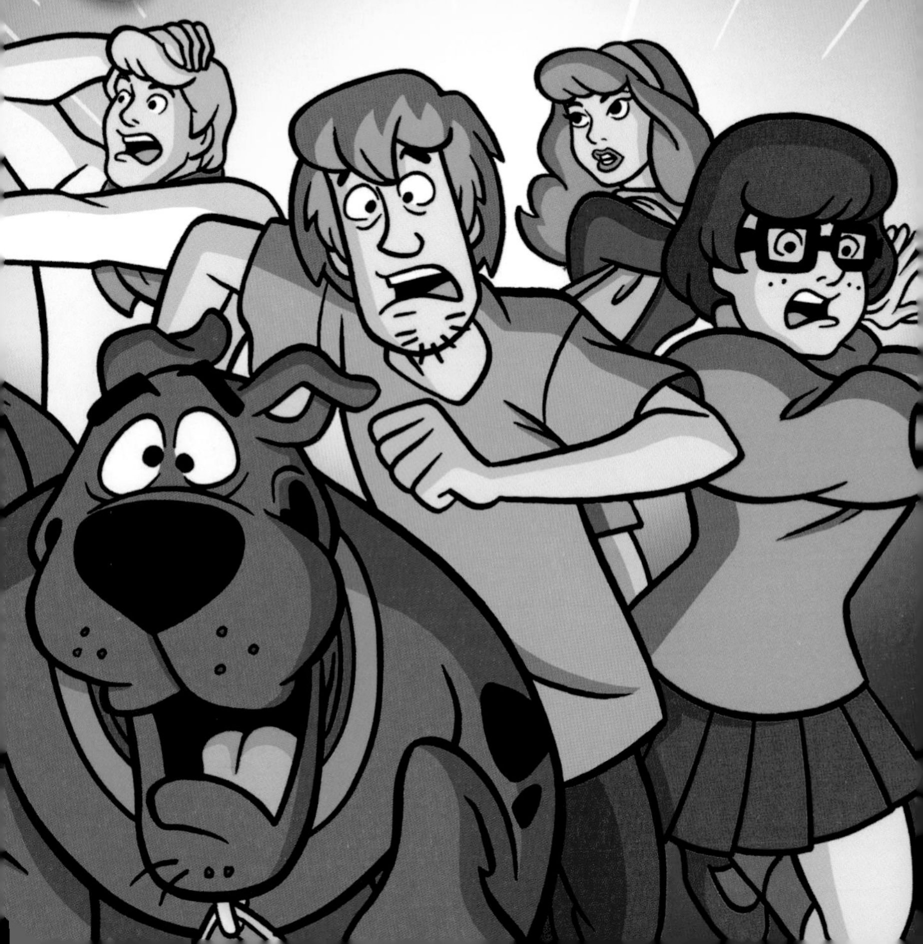

THE CHOICE IS YOURS!

THE FUN DOESN'T STOP HERE!

DISCOVER MORE AT...

www.CAPSTONEKIDS.com